# Hans Christian Andersen's
## Fairy Tales

For Ben and Jessica—M.W.

For Sam and Grace—E.C.C.

Sandy Creek
NEW YORK

An Imprint of Sterling Publishing
387 Park Avenue South
New York, NY 10016

SANDY CREEK and the distinctive Sandy Creek logo
are registered trademarks of Barnes & Noble, Inc.

Text © 2010 by Martin Waddell
Illustrations © 2010 by Emma Chichester Clark

First published in 2010 in Great Britain by Orchard Books,
an imprint of Hachette Children's Books.

This 2014 edition published by Sandy Creek.

ISBN 978-1-4351-5626-5

Manufactured in Malaysia
Lot #:
2 4 6 8 10 9 7 5 3 1
05/14

# Hans Christian Andersen's Fairy Tales

### MARTIN WADDELL
### EMMA CHICHESTER CLARK

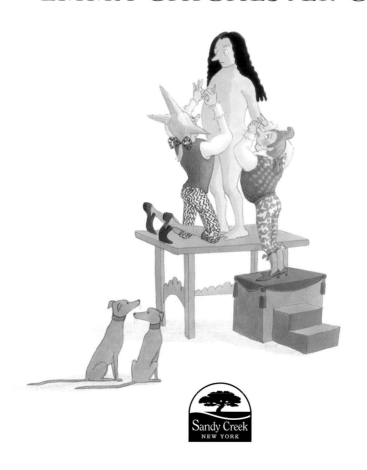

Sandy Creek
NEW YORK

# CONTENTS

# TALES TO BE TOLD

WHAT'S IN THIS BOOK? Stories I loved as a child, and still do.

The scary magic of "The Tinderbox"; the heartbreak and love of "The Little Mermaid"; the playground cruelty and pain of "The Ugly Duckling"; the sadness and injustice of "The Little Match Girl"; the beauty and wisdom of "The Nightingale"; the fun and truth of "The Emperor's New Clothes" . . . They are wonderful tales!

Hans Christian Andersen lived a long time ago, but the questions he raises still challenge the world we live in today—how it could be and should be, and might be, if only we'd listen.

When I was a child, I was told

these stories by people who loved them, each with their own way of telling a tale. My Auntie Bee knew how to play an old witch in a wood, my father could be a dog with huge saucer eyes, my mother could quack the quack of a fondly confused mother duck. Now it is my turn to tell them, in my own way, trying to echo Hans Christian Andersen's voice from the past.

They are stories I love, retold by me, but not mine.

They are Hans Christian Andersen's stories.


MARTIN WADDELL

# A VERY PRINCESSY PRINCESS
## THE PRINCESS AND THE PEA

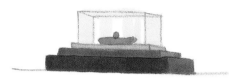

ONCE UPON A TIME there was a prince who wanted to marry a really princessy princess. There were lots of princesses about in those days, so it should have been easy . . . but it wasn't.

Most of the princesses he met were gorgeous looking and had fine clothes and jewels. Nearly all of them knew how to drink tea with one finger crooked very politely. But it takes more than drinking tea politely to prove your princessy princess potential to a prince who is, perhaps, a bit *picky*.

The prince couldn't find one who was princessy enough, and so he gave up, thinking that he'd never marry.

One night, there was a storm. The rain came down in buckets, and someone went *knock-knock* at the door.

The prince opened the door—not very wide, because of the wind and the rain—and in sloshed a soggy princess.

Well, the poor girl *said* that she was a princess. But she had no Royal Umbrella, no Royal Wellington Boots, no Royal Handbag, and why was she wandering about in a storm on her own?

"A real princess? I don't think so!" the queen muttered darkly.

The princess was lovely, but drenched to the skin, and her nose had turned blue. She was coughing a lot, for she'd caught a bad cold in her chest. She called for a hot lemon drink, instead of Royal Gin, and asked for a bed for the night.

"Not *princessy* princess behavior!" decided the queen, taking stock of the sniffing and sneezing princess. "I'll sort this one out with my Real Princess Test."

The queen slipped up to the guest bedroom and took off all the bedclothes and the mattress. She laid a single green pea

on the bed, and then she piled twenty mattresses on top of the pea, one on top of the other.

Then, just to make sure, she laid twenty deep coverlets on top of that, before she put back the sheets and the pillows and blankets.

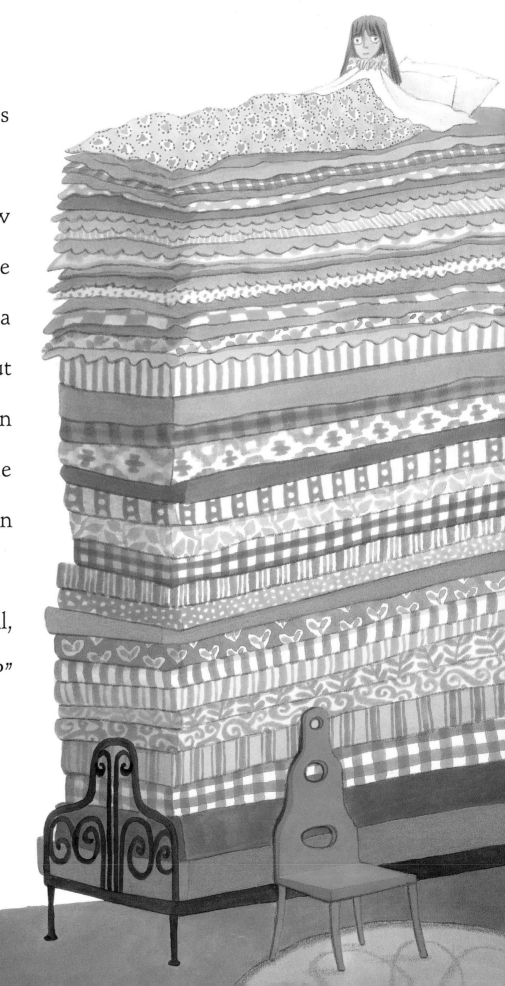

*That* was the queen's Real Princess Test.

I don't know how the princess got into the bed—maybe she used a rope ladder or stilts—but when she came down the next morning the queen asked *the* question that counted.

"Did you sleep well, Your Royal Highness?" she asked.

"Sleep well?" groaned the princess. "I've never laid my Royal Head on a less comfortable bed. I'm bruised black-and-blue, and I've had no sleep at all!"

"Crumbs!" gasped the queen.

"No, ma'am," said the princess politely. "It felt more like a pea."

Only a real princess would feel a pea through all those bedclothes. She'd passed the Real Princess Test.

"Marry me!" cooed the prince, and they were married the very next day, though the prince had to buy a new bed before she would wed—queen-sized, with a no-pea guarantee.

What happened to the *actual* pea? It's in the Royal Curiosity Chest, where the whole world can see it.

That's a princessy princess story about a really *picky* young prince.

Maybe the princess deserved someone better . . . or maybe she didn't.

It depends on what you think of princessy princesses . . . and picky princes.

# AN EGGS-TRAORDINARY EGG

## THE UGLY DUCKLING

THERE ONCE WAS A DUCK . . .

Now that's a good way to start a duck story!

She was a mother duck, and she sat minding her eggs, while the other ducks quacked and swam.

Then . . .

*C-R-A-C-K!* One egg broke.

Out popped a duckling as lovely as only a new baby duckling can be. The mother duck started quacking to tell all the others her baby had hatched.

Then . . .

*CRACK CRACK! CRACK CRACK!*

More eggs broke, and out of the eggs came little plump ducklings with very small legs. One egg was left, an egg that was just a bit bigger than all of the rest.

The egg cracked at last, and out came . . .

. . . a duckling so *odd* that it didn't look like a duckling at all. It was too big for a start, with a long neck and large webby feet. Its feathers were dowdy and gray.

The other ducks waddled up for a look.

"Oh, dearie me, no!" muttered one duck.

"Look at that long skinny neck!" quacked a second duck.

"Call that a duckling?" gasped a third duck.

"He's really *quite* handsome, I think, well *sort of* good looking anyway, or he will be one day," the mother duck quacked, as she cuddled her odd little duckling.

"He'll never be *ducky* like us!" the other ducks said, turning their heads away.

"Never mind, dear," the mother duck told the odd duckling. "We'll show them all when you grow bigger."

18

That didn't help much. The odd duckling's problem was that he was bigger *already*. Bigger and much more awkward than any duckling could or should be.

"Ugly! Ugly! Ugly!" the other ducks quacked, when he waddled down to the mud at the edge of the lake.

"Clear off or we'll bust you!" the biggest duck warned.

The odd duckling wandered sadly away from the lake.

"Thank goodness he's gone," the other ducks quacked, but they couldn't console the duck mother. She searched for days, but she had to give up and admit that her little duck baby was lost.

Where had the odd duckling gone?

He'd found his way to a cottage, where a blind woman

lived, with a cat and a hen.

"A duck?" the blind woman said, feeling his feathers.

She thought from his size that he must be a *very* plump duck, and that pleased her. "That means duck eggs!"

She looked after him and she waited for duck eggs to come, but weeks went by and there were no eggs.

"No eggs!" grumbled the hen.

"Can't purr or catch mice!" muttered the cat.

"What use are you anyway?" the hen asked the odd duckling.

The odd duckling thought for a bit. "I'm amazing on water! I can dive right down to the lake bottom!" he said.

"We don't think much of swimming," the hen told him coldly. "There must be some way you can be of use to the old woman."

"I don't know what I could do!" the odd duckling admitted.

"Ugly *and* stupid!" hissed the cat. "If you can't earn your keep here, you should go."

"They're right! I *am* ugly and stupid!" thought the odd duckling.

He left the old woman's cottage. He just wandered away, not knowing where he was going, or where he belonged, if he belonged anywhere.

Just then some wild swans rose up over the lake, and something stirred deep, deep inside the odd duckling. They were lovely, so *lovely*, those birds.

"Not ugly and stupid, like me!" the odd duckling thought sadly.

How he loved their white-as-snow feathers, their long slender necks and their gracefulness. Tears came to his eyes, though he didn't know why he was crying.

Summer passed into autumn and the beautiful swans flew away to the sun and warm places. Then winter came, and the snow left the lake all aglitter with silvery ice.

Cold, cold, cold . . . and no food. The odd duckling grew, but he grew weak and thin, because there was nothing to eat and he had no mother to help him.

Somehow he lived through the rest of that harsh freezing winter and grew. Every day that he grew, he became more like he-didn't-know-what . . . Whatever it was, it wasn't a duck.

When springtime came and the wild swans returned, he heard their soft call.

It seemed they were calling to him, but they couldn't be, because he was ugly and odd.

"How I wish I was one of those beautiful birds," he thought, bowing his head. Then he looked at his reflection in the water and saw . . .

. . . that his wish had come true.

"That's me!" he whooped. "I'm a swan. I'm a *beautiful* swan. I'm not an odd duck at all."

"Wait for me!" he called to the other swans, and he spread his snow-white wings and rose over the lake to fly with his friends.

The mother duck quacked with delight when she saw him glide over the lake full of beauty and grace.

"There goes my boy!" she told all the others, bursting with pride. She wasn't quite right, but I don't think that matters.

His egg *must* have been a swan's egg that was somehow mislaid. That doesn't say much for the swan who mislaid it, though it says a lot for the duck mother who loved her odd duckling to bits.

Now that's a good way to end a duck story!

# A THREE-DOG TALE
## The Tinderbox

LEFT RIGHT, LEFT RIGHT, LEFT RIGHT, a soldier marched down the road. He had good boots, but no money.

A wicked witch sat by an old gnarled tree. She was flabby and warty and ugly . . . as witches are in most fairy tales.

"Do one thing for me, and your fortune is made, my brave soldier!" the witch greeted the soldier.

"I thank you for that, ma'am," said the soldier politely. He knew he could end up dead or turned into a frog if he angered the witch, so he decided to do as she told him and hope for the best.

"This tree is hollow inside," the witch told him. "There's a hole at the top where you can get in. I'll give you a rope. Tie it around your waist, and I'll lower you down inside the tree. You'll find yourself in a great hall lit by a hundred bright lamps."

"What am I to do when I get there?" the soldier asked, taking hold of the rope.

"There are three locked doors. Unlock the first door

and go in. You'll find a chest guarded by a fierce dog with eyes as big as dinner plates," the witch told him.

"How fierce?" the soldier asked nervously.

"A *brave* soldier like you has nothing to fear from a dog," the witch said. "You'll have my apron with you. Just place it on the floor and set the dog on it. Then open the chest. It is full of good copper money. Take as much as you please . . . though you might prefer silver of course."

"What if I do?" asked the soldier.

"If it is silver you want, go through the second door," the witch told him. "The dog there is much, much bigger. It has eyes as big as mill wheels, but you need not be scared. Just do as you did before, and take all you want. Of course, if gold suits you better, you should unlock the third door. You'll find a giant dog there with each eye as big as the moon.

Place it on my apron, open the chest and you're rich!"

"What must I do for you in return?" the soldier asked carefully. He knew there must be a catch.

"My dear old grandmother Hooktooth left her tinderbox down there," the witch sighed. "I'm too old and bone-sore to squeeze down and get it. Bring it to me. When you find the tinderbox, tug on the rope, and I'll pull you back up."

The soldier scrambled down inside the hollow tree with the rope around his waist, clutching the witch's apron.

Everything in the great hall was as the witch had said it would be. He turned the key in the first door, and unlocked it.

The fierce dog with eyes as large as dinner plates sat there on top of the chest it was guarding.

"Good dog!" said the soldier, and he placed the dog on the witch's apron. Then he opened the chest, and took all the copper money he could fit into his pockets.

"I managed that well," thought the soldier. "Maybe I ought to try for the silver instead?"

In the next room, the much larger dog, with eyes as big as mill wheels, glared at him, looking as though it might tear off his head. The soldier did as before with the apron. Then he threw all the copper money away, filling his pockets with silver . . . but the thought of the gold changed his mind.

"That worked, so why shouldn't I swap my silver for gold?" the soldier thought, unlocking the door of the third room.

There stood a huge dog with great moon-yellow eyes. They spun around like wheels as the dog stared at him.

"There now, good chap!" the soldier said, patting the dog. He placed it on the apron and opened the chest.

Soon his pockets were full of gold coins, and so were his knapsack and cap and his good boots, which he strung round his neck by the laces.

"Pull me up!" shouted the soldier, tugging on the rope.

He could barely move for the weight of the gold, and he clinked and chinked when he did.

"Have you found my tinderbox?" the witch called down the tree. "No tinderbox, no pulling up! The tinderbox is what matters to me!"

"What a special tinderbox it must be," thought the soldier, but when he found the tinderbox it didn't look very special at all.

The witch pulled the soldier up, and he climbed down the tree to the ground.

"Give me my tinderbox!" crowed the witch.

The evil look in her eyes made the soldier sure she would kill him when she had the box in her hands.

"Not so fast! Answer me one question first!" he said, thinking quickly. "What use will you make of this old tinderbox?"

"I'm not telling you that!" snarled the witch angrily.

"Tell me, or I'll cut off your head," the soldier said, drawing his sword.

"You wouldn't dare!" the witch sneered.

So he cut off her head—just like that. You don't dally with a witch.

The witch hadn't told him what
the tinderbox was for, or how to use it,
but at least he'd escaped with his life, and the gold, so the
soldier was pleased.

He slipped the tinderbox inside his shirt and set off
to town, clinking his way down the road.

Soldiers and their money are easily parted, and that
is what happened, of course.

The soldier bought himself rich clothes, and set up as
a gentleman in a grand mansion with a butler and servants.
He was the talk of the town. He made lots of new friends
who told him what a fine fellow he was while they helped

him spend all his money. The soldier was a generous man, and he knew what it felt like to have nothing, so he gave the poor children he met almost as much as he spent. Soon all his gold had gone.

That was a sad day for the soldier.

He had to dismiss his butler and his servants and sell his grand house. He moved into a grubby attic. Maybe his new friends couldn't manage the rickety stairs, or somehow they'd lost his address . . . but they didn't call any more.

One cold night, the soldier sat alone in his dark room, shivering with cold.

He remembered the short stub of a candle he'd seen inside the old tinderbox.

"At least I'll have light to starve by, and some heat . . . though not much," thought the soldier. He struck the flint on the steel in the tinderbox, hoping he'd raise a spark to light the small candle stub.

*FLASH! BANG!*

The door of his room flew wide open. In walked the dog with eyes as big as dinner plates.

"What is your wish, Master?" it asked.

"Bring me more g-g-gold!" the amazed soldier stammered hopefully.

And the dog did.

"Now I know why the witch wanted the old tinderbox!" the soldier thought, patting the dog. "The tinderbox can grant wishes!"

The soldier soon found that striking two sparks brought the dog with eyes like mill wheels, and three sparks brought the giant dog with each eye as big as the moon. They'd blink their huge eyes and bring him whatever he wished for, whenever he asked.

The soldier moved to another grand house, and all his fine friends told him how much they had missed him.

What happened next?

Well, there was a princess. (There always is.) Her father, the king, had locked the princess up in a copper castle. He'd been warned that one day she would marry a soldier, and he didn't like that one bit. People said she was as beautiful

as the moon and stars but no one really knew what she looked like, for no one was allowed in to see her except her mother, the queen.

"I wish I could see that princess!" the soldier told the dog with eyes as big as dinner plates.

The dog was off in a flash. He soon returned, with the princess asleep on his back.

The stories the soldier had heard were all true. The princess was so beautiful that he fell in love at first glance. He couldn't resist stealing just one kiss, though he took care not to wake her, before the dog carried her back.

The next morning, the princess told the queen she'd dreamed

that she'd ridden on a dog's back and been kissed by a soldier.

"A *soldier* . . . I wonder?" muttered the queen, with a frown.

That night, she sent her old lady-in-waiting to sit by

the bed and watch the princess as she slept, just in case.

The dog with eyes as big as mill wheels appeared at

midnight, and bounded off with the princess on his back.

The old lady couldn't keep up with the dog, but she saw the

house he ran to. She chalked a big X on the door of the house, so

it could be easily found the next morning.

At break of dawn, the king and the queen and their soldiers came to capture the soldier.

"Here's the house!" said the king, when he saw an X chalked on the first door they came to.

"No, my dear, it's this one!" said the queen, pointing to the next door. It had an X chalked on it too and so had every other door in the street. The dog with eyes like mill wheels had outwitted the king and the queen, after he had returned the princess to the castle.

The queen had a good brain, and she used it the very next night.

She tied a bag filled with buckwheat to the sleeping princess. Then she nicked a hole in the bottom of the bag. If the girl left her bed, the buckwheat would trickle out and leave a clear trail behind her.

That night, the dog with each eye as big as the moon carried off the princess. The buckwheat trickled out, but the dog didn't notice.

The dog carried the princess back to the castle, just as before. But next morning, the king's men followed the trail of buckwheat to the soldier's front door, and the soldier was arrested and cast into jail.

"You'll hang for this!" he was told.

The soldier was in despair, but . . . one of the poor children he'd helped passed by the window of his cell.

"Fetch the tinderbox you'll find in my house and I'll give you a shilling, my friend!" the soldier called through the bars.

"You were kind to me once, sir, so I'll do it for nothing!" the poor boy told him, and he fetched the tinderbox for the soldier.

"If you won't be paid, take the shilling for luck!" the soldier insisted, and the poor boy went off with the shilling.

The whole town assembled, together with the king and the queen and their counsellors, as the drums beat and flags flew. The common soldier who had dared kiss a princess stood on the scaffold, facing death.

"Wait!" the soldier called to the king, as the hangman put the rope around his neck. "As my last dying wish, allow me one puff of my pipe."

"Of course, such a wish must be granted!" the queen whispered to the king.

"No tricks!" warned the king, as the soldier took out his pipe and tobacco.

The soldier pulled the tinderbox out of his pocket and struck it, as though he was going to light up his pipe.

One spark . . . then two . . . then three sparks together. And the three dogs appeared.

"Save me!" the soldier commanded.

The huge dogs frightened the king and the queen and all their counsellors, and scared all the people to bits.

"Call the dogs off! Be our king! Marry the princess!" the people cried to the soldier.

The princess was brought from the copper castle at once. She'd always hoped she might marry a soldier, and that's what she did, now that she had the chance.

The three dogs were honoured at the royal wedding feast. They stood by the table and stared at the guests with their huge goggly eyes.

I don't know if it's true . . . but I'm told they were wagging their tails.

# THE LITTLE GIRL IN THE SNOW
## THE LITTLE MATCH GIRL

OH, THE LITTLE MATCH GIRL WAS COLD!

It was New Year's Eve, and light glowed in the windows of the rich people's houses around her. The smell of good food filled the street, but she'd eaten nothing all day, not one bite.

The little girl had bundles of matches to sell, but no one came near her to buy them, and she was afraid to go home. She had sold so few matches that she thought that her father would beat her, and so she stayed out in the snow, too cold to weep. The snowflakes glistened on her hair, gleaming like beautiful jewels, though jewels meant nothing to her.

She curled up by a house wall, her feet underneath her for warmth, though there was no warmth in her body. Her bare feet were as cold as the snow.

Then . . . the little match girl struck a match.

*Scratch!*

How it sparked, how it flamed, how it glowed!

She dreamed she was by a warm stove, with brass knobs that gleamed in the light of the flame . . . but then the flame died, and the cold flooded around her again.

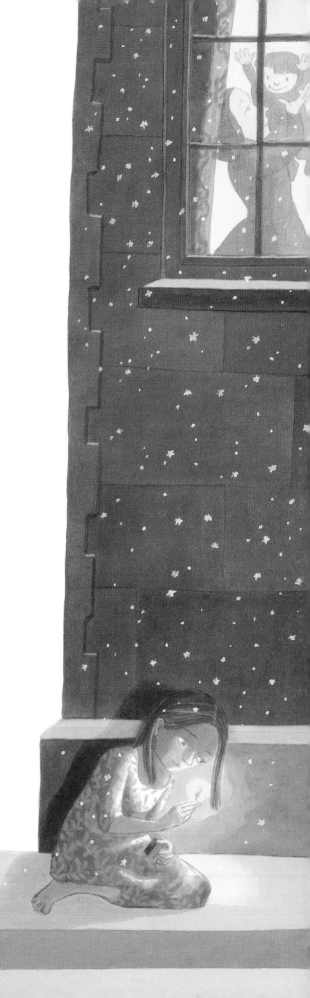

She struck another match.

*Scratch!*

The light on the wall seemed to shimmer and she looked through the shimmer and into a wonderful room, where a table was laid with a roast goose and fine food. The smell of a feast was all around her . . . then the match flickered out, and the roast goose was gone, and so was the warmth of the room.

Another match. *Scratch!*

There was a beautiful Christmas tree, lit with candles. The girl stretched out her arms to the tree, but the lit candles soared into the dark sky above her and became tiny stars.

As the match flickered out,
one star fell from the
sky, leaving a
bright trail
behind it.

"Someone is dying," she thought, for her grandmother had

told her, "When a star falls, a soul rises to God."

*Scratch!*

Another match, and there stood the grandmother who had

loved her so much, wreathed in beauty and smiles.

The little match girl thought that her grandmother would

disappear like the stove and the goose and the Christmas tree,

so she quickly lit all the rest of the matches. They burned with

a light as bright as daylight.

"Oh, take me with you!" the little girl cried.

The old woman gathered the child in her arms. Together they rose in the wonderful light, through the dark night to the stars. There was no cold and no fear any more.

In the morning, the girl's frozen body was found, still sitting there by the wall. There was a smile on her lips and a pile of burnt matches beside her.

"She lit them to keep herself warm as she died, poor little thing," people said. "How sad."

Then they got on with their business, because they had business to do. No one knew her. No one knew of the joy that the New Year had brought or the wonders the little match girl had seen.

The little match girl wasn't cold any more.

She was loved.

# THE GOLD PANTALOONS
## THE EMPEROR'S NEW CLOTHES

THERE WAS ONCE AN EMPEROR who loved beautiful clothes. He dressed in velvet, soft satin, silk and fine lace with most elegant trimmings. Sometimes he shone like the sun, sometimes he glowed like the moon, and even on bad days he sparkled and twinkled.

"My people expect me to look grand!" the Emperor boasted.

The Emperor's wardrobes overflowed with long swirly cloaks, bright-colored shirts, waistcoats galore and fantastical socks. Of all the clothes he owned, the clothes he loved best were his gold pantaloons, which kept him warm in the winter.

Two clever tricksters heard of all this.

"This is our chance to make money, big time, guaranteed!"
they told each other.

They went to the palace.

"We make the most *wonderful* clothes," the first trickster said. "No clothes like ours have ever been seen. The cut and the stitching . . . *nothing* could be finer. And the colors, sire! Our colors are divine, like a meadow of sweet flowers in June!"

"But even better, Your Imperial Highness!" said the second trickster. "The clothes that we make have a magical quality. Stupid people look at our clothes, and see nothing at all!"

"There are no fools at my court!" the Emperor laughed. "At least, I hope not!"

"A glorious thought, Your Imperial Highness!" the first trickster said, bowing low. "But if there *were* any fools at your court, surely you would want to know?"

"Why, yes, of course! And I'd sack them at once!" the Emperor said.

He ordered a set of the wonderful clothes to be made for his next Promenade Day, when he would walk the Imperial Mile, and show himself to his people. A room in the palace was set aside for the work.

"We must have golden thread for weaving our fine fabric!" the two tricksters ordered. "The best there is for the Emperor, thread made of the finest soft silk. And four hundred pearls for the collar of the Imperial cloak."

When the thread and the pearls came, the tricksters slipped them into their bag.

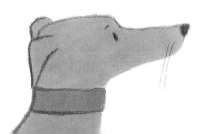

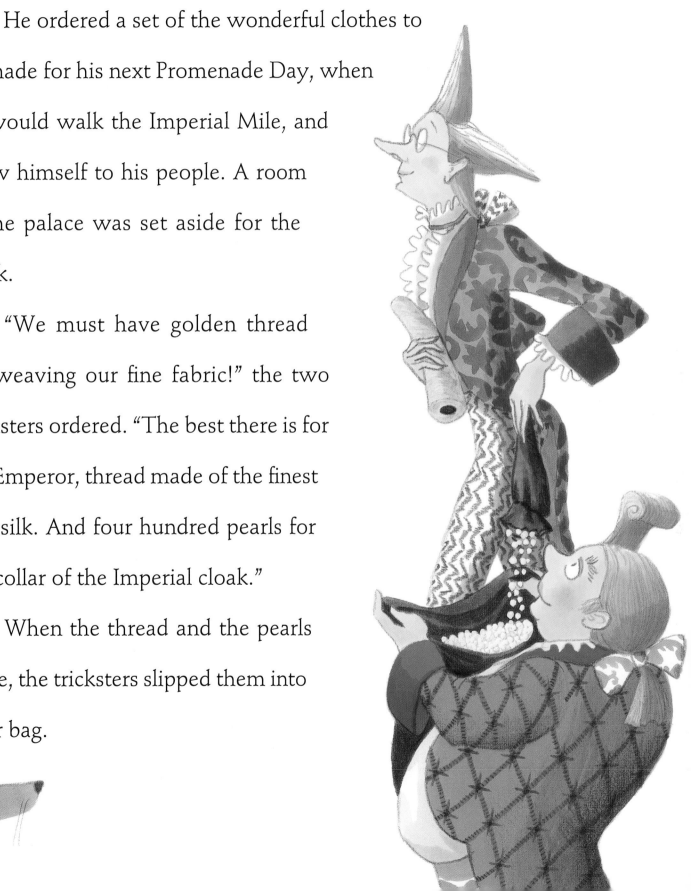

Soon the looms were clanking, and the tricksters were teasing and twisting and twirling, pretending they were teasing and twisting and twirling fine threads, although all the fine threads were hidden away in their bag, with the pearls.

Whispers of the wonderful clothes spread. Everyone wanted to see them.

"I wonder how they are getting on with my new clothes," the Emperor thought. "I must take a peek!"

Then he thought again. Emperors always think twice.

"Suppose for some *silly* reason I couldn't see my new clothes?" he worried. "People might think I was stupid. I'd better send someone else just in case!"

So he sent his chancellor to the loom room in his place.

The chancellor looked and saw . . . Nothing at all. No thread on the loom and no wonder-cloth, because, of course, there was no cloth to see.

His face went bright red, and after that he went white.

"I can't see anything," he thought, "but I can't say that! If I do, the Emperor will think I'm stupid!"

No chancellor can afford to look stupid.

"Glorioso! Fantastico! Quite stupendously fine!" he cried, hurrying out of the room.

"I've . . . er . . . seen nothing like your new clothes before," he told the Emperor carefully. "They are . . . What can I say?

How can I find words to express it? Highness, I'm speechless . . . The quality is . . . Well, you should see for yourself."

"I will!" the Emperor thought.

Then he thought again. Smart emperors always think twice.

"Suppose I can't see what my chancellor saw?" he thought. "That would be a disaster. I'd better send someone else, just to make double sure."

So he sent his prime minister to look at the clothes.

The prime minister peered into the room. He took off his glasses and cleaned them. Then he rubbed his eyes, and put his glasses back on . . . But, of course, he saw no fine clothes, because there were no clothes to see.

"What's wrong with my eyes? Why can't I see what the chancellor saw?" he thought. "The Emperor will think I'm stupid!"

No prime minister can afford to look stupid.

"Bellissima! Splendicious! Delightful!" he cried, and he hurried out of the room.

"Your new clothes, sire?" the prime minister told the Emperor. "I never saw any so fine. I can't wait to see how Your Highness will look dressed in such wonderful clothes."

"That's two men I trust praising my wonderful clothes," the Emperor mused happily. "Sounds good to me!"

The whole town buzzed with the news of the wonderful clothes. Promenade Day came at last, and the two tricksters came to the Emperor's dressing room.

"Your Imperial Highness . . . behold wonders!" they said cunningly. "The cloak! Oh, such style! The elegant doublet . . . the shimmering scarf . . . the fringe of fine lace and the frippets! The sheen of the pearls on the collar! The fabric so soft you can't feel it."

"Amazing!" the prime minister said.

"Superb!" the chancellor murmured.

The Emperor went very pale.

Of course, he saw nothing at all, but . . .

no emperor can afford to look stupid.

There was only one way out

of the mess he was in, so he took it.

"They are the Most Wonderful Superb Extraordinary Delightful and Well-fashioned clothes ever made for my Imperial Self!" he managed to gasp. "I'm flabbergasted! I just can't find words to describe them!"

"We thought you'd say something like that," the two tricksters smiled.

They helped him put on his new clothes, buttoning invisible buttons and smoothing invisible sleeves.

"Astonish yourself, Your Imperial Highness!" the two tricksters cried, as they set him before the Imperial Mirror.

The Emperor looked in the mirror and saw . . . Well, he saw what he saw and he had to think fast.

"Perhaps I should wear some of my old things as well?" he suggested. "Just slip on a pair of my gold pantaloons? You know I like them a lot."

"Alas, Highness, no! We can't grant your Imperial Wish,"

the two tricksters sighed. "That would ruin the line of our wonderful clothes."

That was the end of the gold pantaloons.

The whole court paraded out of the palace, down the great steps to the Imperial Mile, with the Emperor at their head, in his wonderful clothes.

The crowd stood stunned for a moment or two. Then they started to cheer and clap the Emperor's wonderful clothes. Everyone *saw* them of course. No one could afford to look stupid.

But one little boy looked, and then looked again, as little boys do.

"Mommy," he said. "Our Emperor has no clothes on!"

"Shush, dear!" said his mother. "If people hear you say that, they'll think you're stupid!"

A woman started to laugh.

"The Emperor's wearing no clothes!" a man shouted.

"No clothes! No clothes! No clothes!" the crowd chanted. "Our Emperor's wearing no clothes!"

What could the Emperor do? Clothes or no clothes, he thrust his chest out and marched on, head held high, as a great emperor should, all the way down the Imperial Mile.

Which goes to prove there is more to an emperor than his clothes, even an emperor who loves his own glittering gold pantaloons, and wears them whenever he can.

Which isn't always, of course.

# A LITTLE LOVE STORY

## THE TIN SOLDIER

"TIN SOLDIERS!" the little boy shouted, when he opened his birthday present.

He took the soldiers out of their box. They wore brightly painted in red and blue uniforms and all looked the same, except for one soldier. The man who made them had run out of tin, so the last soldier had only one leg.

"He lost his leg doing his duty!" the boy's father told him. "As his general, you should take special note. He's a hero!"

The tin soldier felt proud-to-bursting, though he took care not to show it.

"Guard the palace!" the boy-general ordered, and he set the soldiers up in a line before the palace that stood on the table.

The palace was exquisitely made. It sat by the side of a lake made of glass, where toy swans floated. The front door was wide open, and in the porch a tiny dancer made from paper stood posed on one leg with her other leg held out behind her, as though she was dancing in *Swan Lake*. She was beautifully dressed in white muslin with a blue ribbon over one shoulder. Before her, a tinsel rose twinkled, and it seemed as though she was reaching out to touch it.

From where he was standing, the tin soldier couldn't see the leg that stretched out behind her. He thought she had only one leg, like him.

"That's the wife for me!" thought the tin soldier. "Though I'm only a soldier, perhaps I can hope?"

When the boy-general ordered them all to dismiss and put the tin soldiers away in their box, one soldier was missing.

The tin soldier lay behind a snuffbox that sat on the table, among the other toys there, waiting for his chance.

Later that night, while the house slept, the toys came to life.

They talked and played games, but two of the toys didn't play. The tiny dancer stayed posed on tiptoe, and the little tin soldier was still on duty, guarding the palace, so he couldn't move.

He wished that the dancer would look at him.

Maybe she did, maybe not.

Then . . . the clock on the mantlepiece struck midnight, and up flew the lid of the snuff box. A tiny black goblin with fiery red eyes popped out.

"Tin soldier! Don't hope for what does not belong to you!" he hissed.

The tin soldier ignored him.

"Very well!" giggled the goblin. "Just wait and see what the morning will bring!"

The maids came to air the room the next morning, and placed the tin soldier near an open window. *Puff* went the wind—or was it the goblin?—and the tin soldier blew out of the window. He landed headfirst in the street below, and his bayonet stuck in the flagstones, so that he was upside down.

"What would the dancer think if she saw me?" thought the soldier.

The maids rushed downstairs and out to the street, but they couldn't find him. If he'd cried for help, he would have been saved, but he thought no soldier should do that when in uniform, so he didn't.

It started to rain, and the tin soldier got wet, but he bore that bravely too, as he thought a soldier should.

Then two boys came by.

"A soldier!" one said. "Let's make him a boat to sail in."

They made a paper boat and placed it in the gutter, with the soldier propped up in it. The boat was carried away by the rushing water.

"A troop ship!" thought the little tin soldier. "My duty must lie overseas. I wonder if the dancer is missing me?"

Maybe she was, maybe not. The tin soldier didn't know. He just hoped.

The water flowed into a drain, as dark as the tin box he'd lived in. The boat turned and twisted, buffeted this way and that, but still the tin soldier stayed upright and stiff, as a good soldier should.

"The goblin has done this to me!" he thought. "But if the dancer was here, I wouldn't like her to think I was scared."

Up swam a great rat who guarded the drain.

"Show me your passport!" he roared, gnashing his sharp teeth at the little tin soldier. "You've no right to be here with no passport!"

The rushing water swirled the boat past the rat's claws and its teeth. The boat thundered on down the drain away from the rat.

Then a great roaring came.

"What's that? Where am I going now?" thought the soldier, though he still stood at attention.

The boat plunged over a waterfall into a wide canal below and started to sink.

"Farewell, my dancer!" thought the brave soldier, as the water closed over his head.

*Gurgle, gurgle, gurgle . . . SNAP!*

He didn't know it (how could he know?) but the little tin soldier had been swallowed by a fish.

"Where am I now?" thought the bewildered tin soldier, as warm darkness swirled all around him.

"I am a soldier, and a soldier should stay brave to the end!" he thought, though he couldn't help wishing the end could have been different.

"If only she loved me," he sighed.

Then . . . something struck into the fish.

The fish quivered and wriggled and struggled and gasped. Then it lay still for a long, long time, and grew colder inside.

"What's happening to me?" thought the little tin soldier.

There was a silvery flash, and daylight shone in. The fish had been caught, taken home and cut open in a kitchen.

"Mercy me, who is this in the fish?" someone asked, and the tin soldier was lifted out of the fish and laid on a table.

"It's that tin soldier we lost!" another voice said.

The tin soldier was carried upstairs, and placed back on the table by the open door of the palace, where the tiny dancer still stood.

"I'm back!" thought the little tin soldier. "I hope she'll be pleased to see me!"

"The hero returns!" the boy-general's father told him.

But the tin soldier's fine uniform had faded (which isn't surprising when you think of all his adventures) and the boy-general wasn't impressed.

"You're dismissed from my service!" the boy-general snapped, and he tossed the little tin soldier into the fire. Perhaps he believed that the rusty tin soldier would spoil his parade, or maybe the evil goblin whispered something like that in his ear and the silly boy listened.

Flames roared around the tin soldier, who still stood at attention, but not quite as stiff and straight as before, for the flames were melting the tin he was made of.

He held his head high, looking at the dancer.

Maybe she cared, maybe not. He didn't know. He just hoped.

Then something strange happened: someone opened the door and a blast of air blew the tiny dancer off the table, with her tinsel rose. She fluttered down into the fire, beside the tin soldier. She burst into flames, and was burned into nothing at all.

The next morning, in the cold ashes, the maid found a lump of tin in the shape of a heart, with a twist of charred tinsel beside it, all that was left of the rose.

# THE PRINCESS
## AND THE PIGMAN

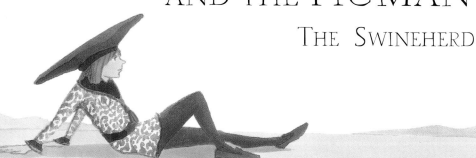

THERE ONCE WAS A PRINCE who thought B-I-G. The time came when he wanted to marry.

"Who should I ask?" wondered the prince.

There were lots of pretty princesses around who would have jumped at the chance, but he decided to start at the top, with the Emperor's daughter.

"I'm a good-looking prince, so why not?" thought the prince.

Well, he wasn't a very *rich* prince—*that* was why not.

"She might go all gooey-eyed and say yes!" he decided.

How do princes woo? They start off by sending fine gifts.

"My rose bush and my nightingale! What more could any girl ask for!" he thought.

It was true. They were wonderful gifts. The little rose bush blossomed just once in five years, and grew only a single white rose when it did . . . but, oh, what a rose, what a *scent*! The nightingale's song was the sweetest that's ever been heard. It banished all sorrow and grief.

"If I send her those, she's sure to invite me to come to the palace and if this leads to that, I might end up married," the prince calculated.

He packed his two gifts in big silver crates and sent them to her by special messenger.

When the princess saw the first crate, she thought it might be a gold pussycat studded with jewels, or something really special like that.

Out came the little bush with the wonderful white rose.

"How beautifully made," gasped the princess.

"What a wonderful scent!" gasped her ladies-in-waiting.

The princess tried sniffing the rose, but she scratched her nose on a rose-thorn.

"This rose is *real*!" she gasped, rubbing her beautiful nose. "What a disgrace! When one is a princess one expects gifts studded with jewels and cleverly fashioned. One expects more than flowers when one's wooed."

"Disgraceful!" tut-tutted her ladies-in-waiting, shaking their heads in dismay.

"Don't get too upset," the Emperor warned. "I'm sure that the young man meant well. Let's open the other gift he has sent you. It might be better."

"It had better be!" the princess replied, tossing her head angrily.

They opened the crate, and the nightingale sang oh so sweetly inside, hidden away in the straw.

"A musical box in the shape of a beautiful bird!" gasped the Emperor's daughter. "What a novelty! How exquisitely made! How intricate! One could almost believe it was real!"

"It *is* a real bird, ma'am, not a musical box," the messenger said, going pale. "It is our prince's most precious possession."

The princess almost burst.

"Who needs a *real* bird?" she raged.

She wrote the prince a very rude note, which really upset him, but he didn't give up.

"There must be more to the princess than that, for she is, after all, the Emperor's daughter," he told himself.

He did what real princes do when they want to know more about a princess they *might* marry: he dressed up in an old dirty shirt and trousers of smelly moleskin and went to the Emperor's palace, not looking at all like a handsome young prince.

PIGMAN WANTED FOR ROYAL PIGS. APPLY WITHIN.

said a note on the gate.

The prince got the job.

What happened next? Well, one day the princess was out taking the air near the Royal Pigsty (as princesses do) when she heard a musical box strike up a tune that went something like this:

*A jolly old sow once lived in a sty,*

*Three little piggies had she*

*And she waddled about singing,*

*"Umph umph umph umph"*

*While the little ones sang, "Wee wee wee."*

"I loved that tune when I was just a tiny princess!" cried the princess. "Someone ask the pigman what he'll take for his musical box."

A lady-in-waiting put on her Wellington boots. She paddled into the muck of the sty where the pigman was working, holding her nose because of the smell.

The lady-in-waiting came out, changed out of her boots and stood looking flushed.

"Well?" demanded the haughty princess.

"I'd rather not say!" the lady-in-waiting whispered. "Someone might hear."

"Whisper it in my petal ear!" the princess suggested primly.

"He asked for ten kisses!" whispered the lady-in-waiting. "He won't settle for less than ten kisses!"

"*You* give him his kisses!" the princess snapped.

"I would if I could, ma'am," blushed the lady-in-waiting. "But he says he wants ten kisses from *you,* or he's keeping his musical box."

Tut-tut-tut went the other ladies-in-waiting.

Just then the tune started playing again, from somewhere inside the pigsty . . . and the princess liked it so much that she gave in.

"Stand around me so that I can't be seen kissing!" she ordered the ladies-in-waiting.

She gave the pigman his ten kisses and then walked away, clutching the musical box.

After that, one pretty

gift followed another, all cleverly

made by the prince in the sty, when he

wasn't tending the Emperor's pigs.

"One shouldn't be tempted," the proud princess told

herself, but each time she walked past the sty, she ended

up giving the pigman his kisses-for-toys, though each time he

asked for more kisses than he had before.

It was big news around the palace, and the big news

reached the Emperor's ears. He was so angry that he banished

the princess and the pigman.

They wandered away in disgrace, and promptly got lost in a forest. To make things worse, it was pouring rain.

"I got it all horribly wrong!" wept the dripping princess. "I should have married that prince. Then I wouldn't be in this terrible mess!"

The pigman ducked behind a hollow tree. He wiped the pig muck off his face, tore off his wet things and changed into his Handsome Prince clothes (which just *happened* to be in the hollow tree where he'd left them).

"Guess who, Princess?" he said, stepping out.

"My prince has come!" swooned the Emperor's daughter. She had half-hoped he *might* be a prince, you see, because that's how it usually works out.

"No way!" laughed the prince. "You scorned things that mattered to me, but you didn't mind kissing a pigman in exchange for the silly toys that he'd made. You've had your chance . . . there's no way I'll marry you!"

He left her singing *Umph umph umph umph* all alone . . .

Which is a bit sad, I suppose, but *I* think she deserved it.

# SWEET SONG
## OF THE FOREST
### THE NIGHTINGALE

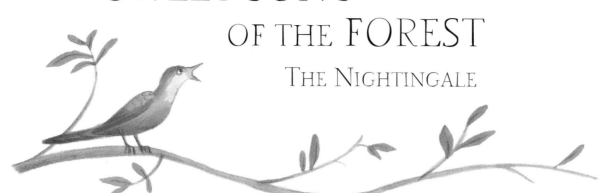

IN THE SOFT TWILIGHT OF SUMMER, a nightingale sang on the branch of a tree. Sweet notes tumbled out of the tiny bird, one after another, in a song full of surprises.

The tree was in a wild forest by the edge of the deep blue sea. Fishermen on the shore stopped to hear the bird sing. As they listened they laughed and smiled, and then they got on with their work, happier than they had been before.

The wild forest was just beyond the boundary of the Emperor of China's magnificent porcelain palace; a palace that was full of the wonders of art, and surrounded by beautiful gardens. Each flower had its own label, handwritten in three languages, and its own little bell that tinkled if anyone touched it. Two hundred gardeners kept the lawns trim and neat, and made sure people kept to the paths.

Poets and writers came from all over the world, and wrote of the wonders they'd seen there. The Emperor was sent the first copy of every book. He read each one with delight, till one day he came upon something that confused him.

"It says in this book that a bird called a nightingale is the most precious thing among all my possessions. But I've never heard of this bird," he thought to himself.

The Emperor summoned his chief minister, the High Panjanderum.

"Why have I never heard of this bird?" the Emperor asked. "She'll sing in my presence tonight, or someone will suffer!"

The High Panjanderum knew who the someone would be, and he quaked inside at the Emperor's words.

"As Your Greatness commands!" he said, bowing low.

It turned out that the High Panjanderum had a problem. No one at the palace had heard of the bird, let alone heard it sing. The courtiers had never been to the forest—there were no trim paths leading through it, and the flowers that grew there had no labels or bells.

At last a shabby little maid in the kitchen spoke up, though she wasn't even supposed to *look* at the High Panjanderum.

"I hear the nightingale's song each day, when I walk to my mother's home in the forest," she said nervously.

"Show us the bird, and you'll be well rewarded," she was told.

The courtiers followed the little maid into the forest, scratching themselves on the brambles. They'd never seen brambles before—brambles weren't allowed in the Emperor's gardens.

*Moo* went her mother's cow.

"That's the nightingale! How sweetly it sings!" they told each other.

"That's just a cow mooing!" the little maid said.

A goose honked, and they thought it was the nightingale, till the little maid told them it wasn't.

"Are you quite sure?" they asked, and the little maid almost giggled.

A frog croaked as they passed.

"How lovely! That must be our bird," the courtiers cried.

"That was a frog," the little maid told them.

This time she couldn't help laughing at the thought of such learned men knowing nothing of frogs, or geese, or brambles or cows.

She brought them to the tree where the nightingale sat.

"Sing!" the little maid told the nightingale, and the small bird sang, oh so sweetly.

"Why, her song is like tiny glass bells tinkling!" the High Panjanderum smiled in delight. "Tonight you shall sing for your Emperor in his palace!" he told the bird.

"My song sounds better in the forest," the bird thought, but that night she sang in the palace. One free-flowing note followed another till tears ran down the Emperor's cheeks, though he didn't quite understand why he was crying.

The nightingale was a great success.

Ladies tried to imitate the bird's song. They filled their mouths with water and gurgled a bit, but it didn't sound right.

Children who couldn't sing one true note were named Nightingale after the Emperor's favourite bird. There were Nightingale Nights, when everyone dressed up as birds . . . How silly can some courtiers be?

All this didn't help the poor nightingale. She was kept in a splendid cage with gold bars. Twice a day she was let out to fly, though she couldn't fly far, for twelve silver strings were tied to her body, and each string was held by a servant.

"Poor little bird!" the little maid thought, for she knew the bird longed to fly freely, though the nightingale was so pleased that she'd been allowed to sing for the Emperor that she never complained.

Then a present arrived from the Emperor of Japan.

It was a gold and silver clockwork nightingale, studded with diamonds and rubies and sapphires. The glittering bird seemed much more beautiful than any real bird could ever be.

"How exquisitely made!" the Music Master purred, as he wound the bird up.

Then it sang, and sang notes so simple and clear that everyone loved it. It's true that it sang only the same waltzes, again and again, but no one minded that—waltzes are easily learned.

"Greatness, this is much superior to the real bird," the Music Master told the Emperor. "Each note sounds exactly as it should. By listening to her, your people will learn the rules of good music. Without knowing the rules, how can anyone tell a good tune from a bad one?"

"By listening to what your heart says," the little maid thought, but what she thought didn't count . . . She hadn't read any books about music.

"The real bird sings whatever notes come into her head," the Music Master said. "You can take it from me, as your Music Master, in musical terms, she's a mess!"

All day, every day, for a week, the glittering bird was wound up and played, while the real nightingale was neglected, but—for some reason he didn't *quite* understand—the Emperor still longed to hear the real bird sing again.

"Let my living bird sing!" the Emperor ordered at the end of the week, but the nightingale's cage was empty, and no one could find her.

"She's no loss to your court, Greatness!" the Music Master said.

The court soon forgot all about the real nightingale. The jewelled one glowed by the Emperor's bed, where it sat on a gorgeous silk cushion.

The Emperor hummed along with the glittering bird while he lay in bed. He knew all the tunes without troubling his mind about whether he liked them or not.

Then something disastrous happened. One night when the Emperor wound the bird up, its clockwork went *clunk* and it whirred, and a loose spring popped out of its back.

"It has been worn out by too much playing," the Imperial Watchmaker explained, when he'd done what he could. "It mustn't be played very often, just once a year or on special days. If it breaks again, I won't be able to fix it."

When the Emperor wound the machine up, it went:

*CLINK! BONK! CLONK!*

very slowly, with an odd added whirr from the workings inside it.

"This is still a fine instrument," the Music Master declared. "The clockwork bird plays very well. Don't be misled by your ears! So long as the notes are played in their correct order, how it sounds doesn't matter a lot."

"Er . . . yes, I suppose so," the Emperor said, and all the courtiers agreed, although one or two of the wiser ones frowned.

"*Clink bonk clonk*?" the little maid thought. "Surely *that* can't be sweet music?"

"Well, it still *looks* wonderful anyway," the wiser courtiers muttered, when they were well out of the Emperor's hearing, and after that the once-a-year bird was left resting on its silk cushion in silence, where it did nothing at all but look good.

Five years passed and the Emperor became very ill.

"He's dying," the High Pandanjerum muttered to the Music Master.

They both hurried out of the palace to seek out the man who would be the next Emperor, to make sure they held onto their jobs.

The Emperor lay in his chamber, alone.

Death came, in his dark cloak, and other strange figures came with him, some beautiful and some ugly. They were the Emperor's good and bad deeds, and Death had brought them to the Emperor's chamber.

They gathered around the Emperor's bed.

"Do you remember us?" they murmured, and their words roared in his head, as they talked of what he had done, or forgotten to do.

"Music, music, play your music for me," the Emperor groaned to the clockwork bird by his bed. "Glittering bird I once loved, drown their terrible words with your song."

The clockwork bird didn't sing. It hadn't been wound up, so how could it?

Death's cold eyes shone greedily as the Emperor's life ebbed away.

Then suddenly, everything changed.

The real nightingale sang on the branch of a tree outside the Emperor's window.

As the nightingale sang, the talking shapes around the bed faded away, and even Death listened, wondering what

beautiful note would come next, until the bird stopped in mid-song.

"Sing on, little bird," ordered Death.

"Grant me the Emperor's life, and I will!" the nightingale said.

"Wish granted, as long as you sing!" Death replied.

The nightingale started singing again and the notes were as clear and as sweet as a bright day in spring.

As she sang, Death kept his part of the bargain and drifted away.

"Your song saved my life," the Emperor told the small bird. "That glittering bird wouldn't sing! I'll break it to pieces!"

"She's broken but she still does her best. And she's beautiful. You mustn't harm her," the nightingale said.

"It will be as you ask, so long as you sing for me every day!" the Emperor sighed.

"I'll come every evening and sing all that I've learned through the day. I'll tell you about the people who are never allowed near your palace, and what they are feeling," the nightingale said. "That knowledge will help you rule. But don't tell your learned officials a little bird told you so. I'm sure they wouldn't like to think that you'd been advised by a small bird who sings on a tree branch outside your window."

And so it came to be. The bird's song told the Emperor of the sadness and joy of his people's lives, and so he learned to look after his people well, as all Emperors should.

The little maid still heard the bird sing every day, as she walked home. One sweet note after another welcomed her back to the soft evening light of the forest.

"How sweetly you sing for us all, nightingale!" the little maid smiled.

And the bird sang.

You might still hear the nightingale's song if you walk in the woods.

If you do, stop and listen.

# DAUGHTER of the SEA

## The Little Mermaid

A ROYAL SHIP LIT BY HUNDREDS OF LANTERNS sailed on a calm sea. There was music and laughter and dancing on board. Fireworks flashed in the sky as the evening star rose.

A dark-eyed prince stood on deck, as handsome a prince as there ever has been. It was his sixteenth birthday party.

A little mermaid swam near the ship. She had a silvery tail, like a fish, and her skin was as soft as rose petals. Her eyes were as blue as the deepest sea.

She had risen from the shimmering world of bright coral

where she lived with her sisters. It was the first time she'd visited the up-above world, and she was enchanted.

Watching the dark-eyed prince, she wished . . . What could she wish? She was the sea's daughter . . . half human, half fish . . . and not of his kind.

The prince saw a shimmer of white foam where she swam. He didn't see the mermaid.

The wind blew softly at first, then it turned to a gale. Lightning flashed, timbers creaked. The wind whipped the sails, and tore them to shreds. The little mermaid loved the power of the sea and she flashed her tail and sang in delight, but the men on the ship were afraid.

Wild waves crashed over the deck, flooding the cabins . . . and the ship sank.

The prince struggled as the waves closed over his head.

"He is too beautiful to die," thought the little mermaid.

She didn't know *why* she should care for the dark-eyed prince who was a child of the land, not the sea, but she did. No one understands love. It just happens. She swam down into the depths and saved her dark-eyed prince. When she reached the shore, the storm had passed and the sun was rising.

The mermaid laid the prince gently on the sand, with his head turned to the sun. She knew that if she stayed in his world she would die, so she went back to the sea, hoping that someone would come to help him.

A beautiful young girl found the unconscious prince, and revived him. She didn't see the watching mermaid,

just a shimmer of white foam near the rocks, as though a small wave had just broken.

The little mermaid returned to her sisters in their coral world under the sea . . . but she was unhappy. She couldn't forget the prince's dark eyes or his beauty. She longed to be part of his strange up-above world and share it with him.

The longing grew too strong for her, so in despair she swam down to the lair of the wicked Sea Witch, deep in the darkest depths of the sea.

Oh, it was horrible there!

Greedy plants reached out to strangle her. Long weeds like oily snakes caressed her beautiful hair. The bodies of sailors twisted and turned in a skeleton dance. There were wounded sea-things all around her, some dead, and some slowly dying, trapped there by the Sea Witch.

"You love the prince and his world!" gurgled the witch. "But humans have souls. When they die, their souls go to heaven. We have no souls. When we die, we fade into white foam that is nothing-at-all, and are gone."

"My grandmother told me a soul would be given to me if I won the love of a human," sighed the mermaid. "But I can't live in their world with a tail . . . "

"You'd swap your beautiful silvery tail for the two stumpy things humans call legs?" crowed the Sea Witch. "I can slice your tail in two with a potion made from my blood. You will

move with a grace that will enchant any human, though each step will feel as though you were walking on daggers. In return I must have your sweet voice. Let me cut out your tongue with my knife, and I'll do as you ask."

"How can I win the prince's love if I cannot speak?" asked the little mermaid.

"Use your wonderful eyes, and your grace as you dance," mewed the Sea Witch. "But remember this . . . if your prince marries another, then at sunrise on the day after his wedding your heart will break. You will fade away into foam that is nothing-at-all."

"I agree," shivered the brave little mermaid. And so it was done. The Sea Witch cut out the little mermaid's tongue. The little mermaid lost her sweet voice and her silvery tail, but she had legs and could walk.

The little mermaid came to her dark-eyed prince with her long hair wrapped around her.

The prince spoke to her gently, stroking her hair. She didn't reply, for she had no tongue, and there were no words she could speak. He led her to his palace, and dressed her in shimmering silks.

The little mermaid danced before the whole court, as no one had danced ever before, swirling and twisting and turning and glancing. Each dainty step filled her with terrible pain, but she smiled for her prince, and danced on and on.

The prince was delighted with her. He called her his little pet, and kept her with him wherever he went. At night she slept by his door.

"You are very dear to me," her prince whispered softly. "You look like the sweet girl who found me alone on the shore when I'd almost drowned. That girl saved my life. I will never forget her."

"It wasn't that sweet girl who saved you...
it was me!" the little mermaid thought sadly.

"Fate has sent you to me to remind me of the
girl that I love," the prince told the little mermaid.
"How I wish I could find her."

The little mermaid's eyes glistened with tears.
One day, of course, the girl came.

She was beautiful beyond a dream . . . even
the little mermaid thought so . . . and the prince
knew he had found his princess.

"I will marry her tomorrow,"
the prince told the little mermaid.
"All I wished for has been
granted. I know you will be
happy for me."

The little mermaid tried to be happy for him, though she knew her heart would break when the sun rose the morning after his wedding day. She would die and fade into foam that was nothing-at-all, as the Sea Witch had warned her.

Dressed in silver and gold, she went sadly to the wedding, and smiled for the prince and his bride.

That night, the wedding party was held on board ship, just as the prince's birthday party had been. The prince and his bride danced, there was music and laughter, and fireworks lit the dark sky. The sea shone with their sparkling light.

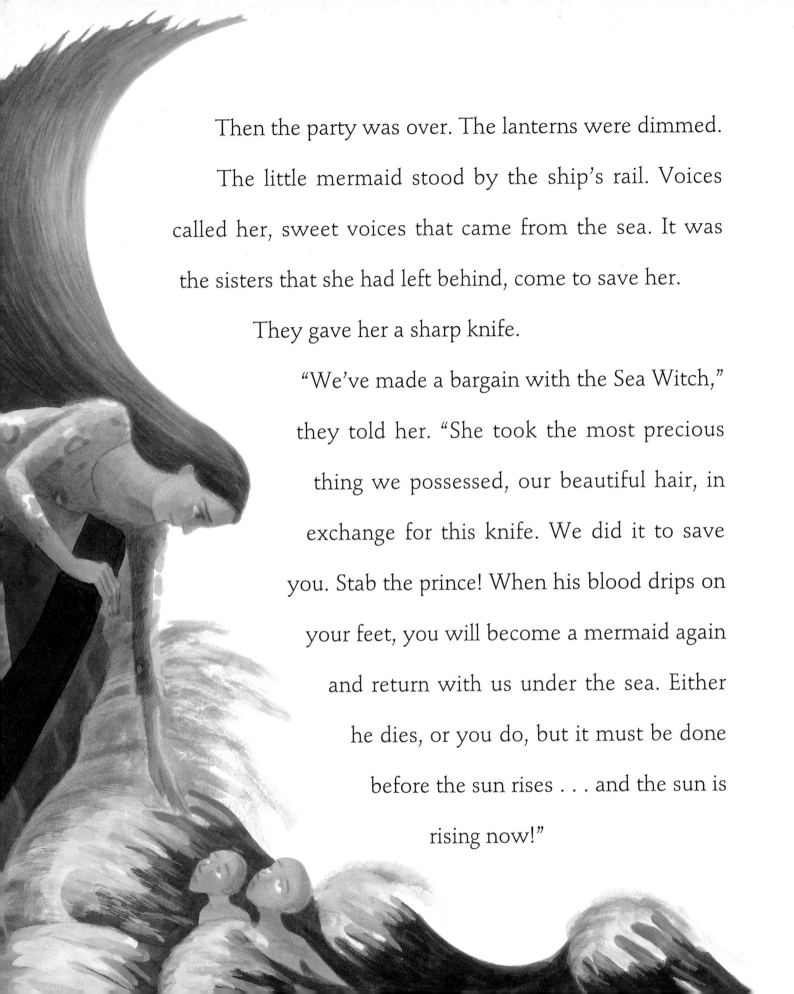

Then the party was over. The lanterns were dimmed. The little mermaid stood by the ship's rail. Voices called her, sweet voices that came from the sea. It was the sisters that she had left behind, come to save her. They gave her a sharp knife.

"We've made a bargain with the Sea Witch," they told her. "She took the most precious thing we possessed, our beautiful hair, in exchange for this knife. We did it to save you. Stab the prince! When his blood drips on your feet, you will become a mermaid again and return with us under the sea. Either he dies, or you do, but it must be done before the sun rises . . . and the sun is rising now!"

With the Sea Witch's knife in her hand, the little mermaid looked down at the prince and his beautiful bride, lying together.

*Either he dies, or you do.*

She raised the Sea Witch's knife.

*Either he dies, or you do.*

The sharp blade stirred in her hand, as though the wicked Sea Witch had twitched it.

*Either he dies, or you do.*

The little mermaid threw the knife from her. The sea churned blood red where it fell.

The sun rose, and the little mermaid faded away in a shimmer of white foam, as the Sea Witch had told her she would.

The foam drifted away in the wake of the ship. But it wasn't nothing-at-all, so the Sea Witch was wrong!

"My heart has broken and my body has gone but, in some way that I don't understand, I live on," thought the little mermaid.

She sparkled and shone in the up-above world, where she had longed to be, part of the sunlight that shines on the sea.

And she's shining still.